SIMPLY NOT ENOUGH

Kelen Tamurian

Elisely
PUBLISHING

Copyright © 2021 by Keira Barr

First paperback edition June 2021.

Book cover artwork by Kelen Tamurian.

ISBN: 978-1-0878-7442-5

Published by Elisely Publishing, Seattle
elisely.com

To all the girls out there trying to love themselves... because that shit is hard. You may have been told you are not enough by society, by somebody you care about, or maybe even by the thoughts in your head.

But you are more than enough... simply because you are.

I'd like to also acknowledge my family, who inspire me to share what is on my heart and have always supported me with unconditional love.

And thank you to my English teacher, Ms. Casey, who created a space for me to explore my creativity, allowed me to bug her with my burning questions, and inspired me to believe in the power of my writing.

Contents

Introduction

Throughout my life, I have strived for perfection and never felt good enough. There was always something I could've done better and there was always something to criticize. I felt nothing was ever good enough, not my grades, my ability to play the sports I loved, or my body. I spent years picking myself apart, wishing I or a grade I got back on a test was different in every which way. And the saddest part was that I thought I was the only one who felt this way. I thought everyone else was comfortable in their own skin because no one ever said anything different. I thought there was something wrong with *me.*

In a society where more is better and perfection is the object we are told to obtain, it felt impossible for me to accept myself as I was and acknowledge that I am good enough. Simply because I am. It felt impossible for me not to want to change the parts of myself that didn't measure up to society's expectations and standards, or to the people around me. I compared every inch of myself to what I thought I should look like, act like, and be like. I spewed words of hatred toward the body that had carried me through every day of my life and only wanted to see me thrive. I ridiculed myself for missing one point on my math test because I thought I should have been able to get a perfect score, something I thought I needed to be smart, worthy, and valuable. I criticized myself down to the way my eyes crinkled when I smiled. Every piece of me was something to condemn, and I couldn't foresee a reality where I could experience anything different.

It wasn't until I caught a glimpse of myself in the mirror where I saw the sadness in my eyes, the fear in my heart, and the shrunken version of myself staring back that I questioned who this belief that I wasn't good enough served. I realized it wasn't serving anyone. It most definitely wasn't serving me. I finally understood that I deserved better. I began to entertain the thought that maybe I was good enough, simply because I was. And when I started to truly believe this, my life changed.

I realized that women feel this need to shrink themselves to fit into society, a tight pair of jeans, or the standards and expectations that others have set for them, and recognized that it was time to stand up and stand out. I started telling myself that I deserved to take up space in this world and that me, my opinions, and my feelings were valid. I told myself that I was so much more than what I thought about myself on my worst days, and that I was worthy regardless of the voice in my head and the voices of others telling me otherwise.

And so, I wrote *SIMPLY Not ENOUGH* to fully encapsulate the journey to discovering and accepting that reality as truth. I wanted to fully express that the feeling of not feeling good enough is so universal and it impacts so many of our lives. You are not alone and there is absolutely nothing wrong with you. I felt called to showcase that this journey of life is not easy and you will hit bumps in your road. But those bumps are what make you resilient, and your resilience will allow you to choose and continue to choose to believe that you are good enough, simply because you are.

SIMPLY Not ENOUGH will show you that you have the power to determine your own reality. You have the power to believe in yourself. But it will not always be as easy as just deciding that you are good enough. You will have to consciously and continuously work to change your thinking, your habits, and your relationship with yourself, as well as your mind and body.

This may sound scary and overwhelming, and I totally understand. I was in the same boat, and that is why I created a community called "Simply Enough" that works to empower its members to show up as their highest selves to understand the value of their presence and the importance of their worth. Through sharing personal experiences, exploring the topics of my book, *SIMPLY Not ENOUGH*, and building a community of women that lift each other up and support each other in times of need, "Simply Enough" strives to change the way women show up in the world.

"Simply Enough" will also provide you with the tools you need to fully begin to accept yourself as you are. You will learn about meditation, journaling, and body acceptance/body neutrality. You will learn how to connect to your inner wisdom and how to heal your past traumas, and most importantly, you will learn to respect your personal journey without judgment for what it looks like compared to the community members around you. You will connect with your authentic self.

You can find more information about this community and how to join through my website, kelentamurian.com.

So, I urge you to turn the pages and connect with the journey weaving its way through them. I hope you feel seen, heard, and inspired. I hope that you begin to choose yourself. And I hope that you begin to choose to believe that you are good enough. I promise that this will be the most fulfilling thing you will ever do.

Am I Enough?

High school is supposed to be picture perfect, right? You know, the greatest time of your life where you find your best friends that you'll have for the rest of your life. You meet your first boyfriend and have your very first kiss. You turn sixteen and find freedom in the form of keys for your first car, and you cruise through life without a care in the world. Right?

I mean, that is what I was expecting. But now that I am here sitting in math class, reminiscing on what could and should have been, I feel empty. I haven't experienced any of these things the way I thought I was supposed to.

I haven't met my "girl tribe," and most days I walk around campus alone in hopes no one will come up and ask how my day is going. Because in all honesty, I don't think they'd really want to hear my answer. And, of course, I can barely muster up the courage to say "hi" to that boy I like. Besides, he has a girlfriend who looks absolutely nothing like me. So, I don't even stand a chance anyway.

And no one told me that driving alone is so unbelievably lonely. I've found there is only so much the lyrics to my favorite songs can do to drown out the voice in my head, telling me that I'm just not good enough. I almost feel like I'm doing this whole thing wrong, you know?

I wake up every morning expecting everything to just change, hoping someone has flipped a magic switch on my life in the middle of the night, and all of a sudden I don't care about what my body looks like compared to the girl standing beside me. And, I don't berate myself with words of hatred about the fact that no matter what I do, I just never feel like enough.

But so far that day has not come, and as I sit here in my creaky uncomfortable chair listening to my math teacher Mrs. Hills call out the names of the students with the top scores from our latest test, I feel even more like a failure in my own life. I wait impatiently for my name to be called out following one of the top scores, but it never comes.

"Everyone else, better luck next time," she says. "I'm going to pass your tests back, and if you have any questions come see me after class," she turns around looking at the clock, "which is in three minutes. I'll be available for you then."

She walks around the room, her face rising and falling with each test she hands back. As she approaches my desk I can see her face contort into an uncomfortable smile with what looks like a hint of disappointment.

"Almost, but not quite," she whispers.

She hands me my test and my eyes dart around the page searching for my score. I find it in the top right corner scribbled in small blue ink. 92. An A-.

My heart sinks deep into the hole it has created for itself over the last few years for moments just like this, when my inner perfectionist is left feeling unsatisfied. And I can't bear the shame that follows. I feel hot tears, clawing their way out from my eyes as I glance up at the clock, noticing there is only one more minute left of class.

When the bell rings, I wipe my eyes in an attempt to compose myself before walking to the front of the classroom to ask Mrs. Hills about my score. Stuffing my books into my bag, I stand a little too quickly. My chair creaks just loud enough for the entire class to turn around as they walk out of the room.

Just great, I think to myself. Luckily, it looks as though no one else is staying to ask about their score. I quickly walk up to her desk.

"Hi, Mrs. Hills. I have a question about my test. I know the score can't be changed, so I'm not asking for that. But... I was wondering if you have any tips so I can be better prepared next time? I studied a lot for this test and was hoping for a better grade."

"Sure, remind me of your score again?" she asks.

"A 92," I reply.

"Oh my goodness, Hope," she says. "You did just fine. I have noticed that you strive for perfect scores, but you should be very happy with that one. Even though some did well, most did not. So, don't worry about this. I mean, I know a 92 isn't a solid A, but it's good enough."

"Yeah, it was silly for me to even ask for help. Um, I will see you on Monday. Thanks."

"No problem. Bye now."

I hurry out of the room, my thoughts thundering around my brain like the hooves of a horse pounding the dry yellow grass beneath it. My legs suddenly feel as though cinderblocks have replaced my feet, as I desperately try to concentrate on putting one foot in front of the other before the tears fall. One after another.

Stepping onto the path to soccer practice, I notice the greenery that lined it just a few months ago is beginning to wither as it turns into a lifeless brown cover. I see myself in the withering brush. Each time I let the fear that I'm not good enough consume me, I, too, feel withered up into nothingness.

I begin to think about the conversation I just had, and even though my test score was better than some other kids in my class, it doesn't take away my insecurity in my ability to perform. It doesn't take away the pain of feeling unworthy for even being in an advanced math class. It doesn't silence my fear that I will never be enough.

If someone else could hear these thoughts, they would laugh about how ridiculous this is. Because it doesn't even matter. It's just a test score. And yeah, to most people it is just a test score. But to me, it's a declaration of my worth. I pride myself on my ability to perform in school because it's the one thing I seem to excel the most at.

I'm not a first-team All-American lacrosse recruit to Harvard like my brother was last year. I don't have the perfect body type like all the girls on social media seem to. I'm just a girl from Seattle on a high school soccer team, trying to find my place in this world. And unfortunately, that has been a bigger challenge than I had anticipated. Especially when my mind keeps telling me that I'm not good enough. I have to do more. Be better. Be perfect.

Lost in my thoughts, I find myself staring blankly at the girls' locker room doors, and I trace the outline of the royal blue door casing with my eyes. Suddenly, the doors burst open and my teammate Addie is yelling at me to get my butt in the locker room because practice starts in five minutes. I shake my head and rush inside, reminding myself to put on a happy face.

Creating Confidence

As I turn the dial on the combination lock, I realize my happy face isn't working as well as usual. Addie can see right through it.

"Hey, Hope," she says. "What's going on? You look a little down."

"Oh, I'm fine. It's nothing."

"Hope, come on, we've been playing soccer together since fifth grade. I know you. What's wrong?"

"Nothing. Seriously. I'm okay."

"Hope," she sighs and looks up as she finishes tying her cleat. "You have five seconds to tell me what's going on before I make it my mission to kick your ass in practice today."

"You do that anyway, Addie. So it looks like my secret is all mine."

"Oh, shut up," she laughs. "You literally wipe the floor with me in school. I mean, if I got the grades you do my parents would never lecture me again. So, come on. What's up?"

"All right. Well, I just had a hard conversation with my teacher that kind of rubbed me the wrong way, I guess," I finally answer.

"Was it with Mrs. Hills? She can rub anyone the wrong way. I swear, the way she smiles at you while giving you bad news about your math homework or test is honestly terrifying."

"Yeah, it was," I laugh. "I wanted to ask her for some help with studying tips to improve my test score for next time..." Addie cut me off abruptly.

"Wait, wait, wait. What did you get on the test? It was probably an amazing grade that doesn't need to be improved."

"I got a 92. So an A-."

"Exactly. Hope, that is such a good score. Why do you even feel the need to change it? If I got grades like that on my math tests I would be so happy!"

"Oh, thanks. Um, yeah. That's kind of what Mrs. Hills said too. She told me not to worry about it, and just sent me on my way."

"Hey, I mean if your teacher tells you that you got a good grade then that is all you need to know to move on and be happy with it," she looks up at the clock. "Hope, we've got to go! Practice starts in two minutes!"

"Okay. I'll meet you out there, I need to grab a headband."

As Addie runs out the door I become lost in my thoughts again. This is why I don't tell people about stuff like this, they just don't understand. I mean, sure Addie might feel pressure from her parents to do better in school. And I'm sure that's really hard. But does she also have a constant voice in her head dictating whether she looks good enough, or simply is enough? I mean, no one ever talks about this. Why is that?

I try to shake everything off so I can fully focus on practice. We are about to go into the third round of playoffs for the state championship, I have to be on my A-game. I step outside and a balmy dew floating through the afternoon air tickles my cheeks as I run towards my teammates huddled in the center of the field.

The bright green grass squeals and squeaks below my cleats as water seeps in. Approaching my teammates, I sense exciting trepidation in the air for the practice ahead and hear my coach's voice begin to bellow among us as he rolls out the agenda for today's practice.

"All right Lady Falcons, organize yourselves into three lines of seven and start your usual drills," he yells. "Once everyone has gone through each drill, we are going to work on some possession and one-on-ones. Then we will scrimmage for the rest of practice to gear up for our first playoff game next week. Sound good?"

"Yes, coach," we reply in unison, as always.

Drills go off without a hitch, everyone is on fire today and I couldn't be happier. My passes are crisp, my touches are light yet powerful, and my head is clear. Finally.

Soccer is one of the only things that will do that for me. I don't know what it is, but it works every time. Maybe it's the feeling of scoring the winning goal for the team. Maybe it's the fact that I know my teammates will always have my back. Maybe it's the fire that is lit up inside my soul each time I touch the ball.

I become alive when I play soccer and it makes me feel like I can do anything. Feeling proud of myself and confident in my ability to play, I laser in on the task at hand, keeping the ball away from Addie at all costs. The whole team knows when Addie gets the ball, there is no stopping her. She will take down anyone that gets in her way. It is both scary and inspiring. My job as the center midfielder is to keep the ball away from her fiery feet, and I know that I can.

This confidence seems out of place among the thoughts rolling around in my head earlier. In fact, it feels so foreign that it makes me nervous because I fear that if it doesn't last I may make a mistake that costs my scrimmage team everything.

I try to shove the fear down as far as I can and refocus my energy on the scrimmage, but it's proving to be difficult. The "what ifs" rise up and cloud the clear blue sky that once occupied my head. The self-doubt twists and turns forming a nasty hurricane that obliterates any sliver of self-assurance I had, and it becomes so wild that it hinders my vision. I don't see Addie effortlessly swoop in on the ball right in front of me, taking it and charging back down the field.

I stand frozen like a dangling icicle, ready to fall and break into a million pieces. I feel so defeated. Not even by Addie, but by myself. The fact that I can let one single twinge of fear dismantle all of my confidence is unnerving. It's the confidence that deep down I know I am worthy of, but can't seem to always hang on to. I look down the field just in time to see Addie score a perfect goal before hearing my coach's whistle.

"Hope, come here." I could tell he was not happy.

"What happened out there?" he spoke carefully as I looked up at him.

"Um, I'm sorry coach. I just spaced out."

"Spaced out? Hope, we are playing to earn a spot in the state championship."

"I know," I look down. "I have had a pretty hard day, and that is not an excuse but I just have a lot going on in my head right now," I say quietly. "I let it get the best of me, I'm sorry."

"Listen, I get it," he softens. "Everyone has those days. But you've got to try to shut it all out, turn down the noise in your head, and focus on what is in front of you. Why don't you take a few minutes off the field to sit and reset, okay?"

"Okay. Thanks, coach."

He nods and looks away as he turns to get the team back into formation for the next play. I can't believe I just stood there and watched as she ran past me and scored a goal. I let my entire team and coach down. And most of all, I let myself down. I walk to the bench and try to distract myself from the embarrassment and disappointment by watching the rest of the scrimmage. The whistle to dismiss us from practice can not be blown soon enough.

About an hour later, the whistle finally blows. After gathering my gear I start walking to my car alone, but Addie sidles up next to me with the biggest smile on her face.

"What's up, Addie?" I ask.

"Oh, nothing. the boy I have been crushing on for a while just smiled at me and told me that I had a great practice."

"Oh my gosh, Jacob?"

"Yes! I can't believe he came to watch us practice today!"

"Aw, yeah, that was nice of him. Hopefully, he didn't see me look so dumb just standing there while you went off and scored a perfect goal."

"Oh, yeah. What happened with you there? I mean, I didn't want to question the fact that you weren't challenging me because, hey, I could go score a goal. But, that was so out of character for you."

"It felt so out of character, but at the same time, it didn't. I was feeling really confident going into scrimmage because I was having a good practice, but then I started doubting that confidence. Then everything just went to shit."

"Why were you doubting that confidence? You created it."

"What do you mean?"

"That confidence doesn't just come out to nowhere, Hope. You create it within you. Your belief in your ability to play amazing soccer is what creates that confidence. So, if you created that confidence, why would you doubt that it isn't supposed to be there?"

"Woah, Addie. That was deep," I chuckle. "When did you become a philosopher? But, I don't..."

"Hold on. Sorry, my mom is calling me. Hello?" she answers her phone.

"It's no big deal, see you tomorrow," I mouth and wave as I start to walk over to my car. Grabbing my keys out of my bag, I unlock the car and go inside, closing the door softly. I sink into the black leather, feeling the coolness soothe my sore legs.

I think more about what Addie said and slowly finish the thought I was about to say earlier, that I don't know if that is true for me. Maybe everything I need is already inside of me, but maybe it isn't. How would I even know?

Coach Told Me So

I take the long way home, drowning out the noise in my head by listening to my favorite songs. The sun slips behind the clouds, blanketing the sky in a quilt of bright pinks and subtle oranges. As I drive up the long steep hill leading to my neighborhood, I look over and notice how the deep blue water of Lake Union is rippling with the rhythm of the wind, as it seems to go with the flow of its surroundings.

Pulling into my driveway, a wave of dread ripples over me. Coming up with an elaborate excuse to hide the fact that today sucked feels exhausting. So, maybe for the first time, I'll just be honest.

Turning off my car, I reach into the back seat to grab my soccer bag and backpack to head inside. As I walk into the house I smell my dad's homemade meatballs and tomato sauce, a recipe passed down from his grandmother that we cherish and look forward to every Friday. Closing my eyes, I breathe deeply, inhaling the scent of the earthy tomato and the heartiness of the meatballs, imagining a bowl full of pasta wrapped in the full-bodied reds and oranges of the sauce. Walking into the kitchen, I open my eyes to find a surprise sitting at the kitchen table. Ethan is home!

"Hey, sis!"

"Ethan!" I scream running over to him, ready to give him the biggest bear hug. Jumping into his arms, taking in the familiar smell of his cologne I am reminded of how much I miss him while he's away at college.

I miss being able to walk through our Jack and Jill bathroom and go into his room to talk whenever I need to vent about life. I miss going on our spontaneous adventures to the mountains or the lake to swim and get ice cream from our favorite shop, Molly Moon's. So being here right now, hugging my best friend in the whole world, is everything.

"I have missed you so much Ethan, you don't even know. It's been so weird driving to school without you and not being able to see you in the halls walking from class to class."

"I have missed you too, Hope. College is cool and all but I haven't met anyone that makes me laugh like you. I'm happy to be home."

"Glad to hear you haven't replaced me yet," I laugh. "So, how's your season going?"

"Well since it's only November, our season hasn't actually started yet," Ethan answers. "We start playing games in February, but right now we are doing lots of scouting, lifting, and watching films to help improve our game. So that has been good. How's soccer? I heard you guys are on track to win the state championship this year!"

"Yeah, we are going into the third round of the playoffs starting Monday."

"Oh wow, well good thing I don't have to go back to school until Wednesday!" Ethan smiles.

"Wait, you're going to be able to come to my game?"

"Only if you'll have me!"

"Yes, of course!" I squeal, turning to hug him again because I am just so happy he will get to watch me play. Ethan hasn't come to one of my games since I was a sophomore, I can't believe it's been a whole year.

"What is all the screaming and squealing about?" Mom asks as she walks into the kitchen with a glass of wine.

"Oh, nothing. I'm just excited that Ethan is home and can come to my playoff game this week."

"Aw, well, I'm glad. Are you guys hungry? Dad will be down in a few minutes, he's just finishing up a call for work."

"Yes, I am starving! Is Dad on-call tonight?" I ask.

"No, but he needed to talk to his colleague about a surgery they are doing together tomorrow."

"Oh, gotcha. Well, I'll set the table so that when he comes down..." I begin.

"So that when he comes down, what?" Dad asks with curiosity.

"Oh, hey Dad! I was just about to set the table so we can eat, we're hungry!"

"All right. Well, let's eat!" We all grab plates from the cupboard and forks from the drawer and dig into the best meal of the week.

Speechless for the first few minutes, as I shovel as much pasta and sauce into my mouth as I can, I listen to my dad talk about the memories he has of cooking with our great-grandmother growing up.

"My nonna started teaching me how to cook when I was just eight," Dad brings us back to his days as a little boy, which for some reason isn't hard for me to envision.

"I would watch her cook our favorite meals and traditional Italian dishes for every holiday and was in awe of how food could bring us together in a way that nothing else could," he continues. "My entire extended family didn't come together very often, unless my nonna facilitated it. And, of course, cooked her delicious food. But, I always appreciated her most for her desire to spend time with us."

"What was your favorite meal she cooked for you?" Ethan asks.

"Definitely her stuffed calamari. I am nowhere near as good of a cook as she was so I don't even dare try and make that dish. I just couldn't do it justice. But, her spaghetti and meatballs was a close second and that is why I make it for you all every Friday, in her honor."

"Aw, I love that Dad," I say with a smile. I know how close Dad was with his grandma and how much he misses her every day.

"So, Hope, how was your day?" he asks me. And there it was, the dreaded question.

"Honestly, it kind of sucked. First, I went to math class, and you know math is my hardest subject, so it's the one I study hardest for. We got our chapter 3 tests back today. I got a 92, so an A-."

"That's not bad Hope," my mom adds.

"I know, but I felt like I should've done better, so I went to ask my teacher about how I can study differently for next time, and she basically gave me the same answer you just did," I say.

"She said my score really wasn't that bad and I should be happy with it because not everyone in the class did as well as I did," I continue. "And while I'm sure that was meant to make me feel better, it actually made me feel worse because I just felt stupid for asking for help and I should've just kept to myself. No one really understands the pressure I put on myself or the way I feel it."

"Well hey, just know there is nothing wrong with asking for help. And you shouldn't feel bad about asking for it, even when the response you get isn't what you are expecting," my mom encouragingly interjects.

"Yeah, that is true and something I should try to remember. Anyway, after math class I went to practice and was feeling really good. My touches were great and my passes were perfect, but I got all up in my head thinking about the day I had and how the confidence I was feeling about my skills didn't feel like it should be there. And so, because I wasn't even focusing on the game in front of me, I let Addie just run on by me with the ball. She scored a goal on my team for the scrimmage. Coach John called me off and asked what happened, and all I could tell him was that I spaced out and I needed a minute. It was so embarrassing and made me feel like a failure."

"That definitely sounds like a rough day," my dad says. "You've never shared anything like this before, what made you want to share it all in this way?"

"I couldn't bring myself to make up an elaborate excuse for why my day was actually okay when it really wasn't." I sigh, a heaviness falls on my shoulders. "I couldn't bring myself to try and act like life is so perfect."

"Hope, you don't have to sugarcoat anything with us," he responds. "We want to know how you are feeling, and we want to know the truth because otherwise we can't be there for you."

"Thanks, Dad," I say as some of the weight lifts off of my shoulders, "Anyway, Addie came up to me after practice and I told her how upset I was with myself and she said something really interesting. She asked why I would even question my confidence... because I create it. That my confidence comes from my belief in myself and my ability to play the sport I love, so why would I question something that comes from a place of pride within me. Her words struck me so deeply, but it feels weird to try to flip a switch and start to believe in myself."

Ethan clears his throat, "Hey, Mom and Dad can I talk to Hope alone for a bit?"

"Sure Ethan," Mom says, and turning to my dad asks, "Honey, do you want to sit on the deck and watch the rest of the sunset?" Dad nods leading her out onto the deck with his hand on the small of her back. *Oh, my parents are so cute*, I think to myself. Turning to Ethan and looking into his caring eyes, I wait to hear what he has to say.

"While I was listening to you talk about your day I noticed that you said that no one understands the amount of pressure you put on yourself, but I just want you to know that I do understand," he says looking back at me.

"You do?" I ask, and look down.

"Yes, I mean I am your brother. Before I left for college I could see how stressed you seemed every day, it looked like you were under a lot of pressure. I also understand because I know how easy it is to put that pressure on yourself and feel this need to be perfect in everything you do. It's really hard. There is this expectation that we all have to do more, be more, be better. But even when we are already trying our best, it never feels like enough."

"Wow Ethan, I never knew you felt this way too, I honestly thought I was alone in this feeling," I say as I continue to stare at my plate.

"You are definitely not alone, let me tell you. I mean, half of my team at Harvard feels this pressure too. We put a huge amount of pressure on ourselves to be the best people, players, and students we can be. And it's hard."

"Yeah, it really is," I say. "It's comforting that others feel this but at the same time it's sad that so many other people feel like no matter what they do, it's not good enough."

"I know, it's a weird feeling. It's like you are happy to know it's not just you, but then you realize, oh shit, it's not just me. Anyway, I want to share something with you."

"Okay, shoot," I pick up my fork and start playing with the last few noodles left on my plate.

"My lacrosse coach told us something before our first practice this season, and it has really helped me deal with some of that pressure. He told us that we are really the only ones who truly care about how we perform. No one else is looking at us through the same lens that we see ourselves through. So, it's all that much more important to believe in yourself, because nobody else is in your head and knows what it's like to be you. He said believing in yourself and who you are is a superpower, and the sooner you recognize it the sooner that pressure sitting on your shoulders like a ton of bricks will begin to lighten. One brick at a time. And he's right. Believing in yourself makes all the difference."

"Wow, I mean everything your coach said is amazing, and now I am realizing two people have said basically the same thing to me. Maybe it's time I listen," I say as I finally look up. "Maybe, believing is the key to everything in life, and maybe I need to try it out."

"You know what, it really is," Ethan smiles. "By changing your self-talk about not being good enough, your fear will start to fade away, I promise. But, this is not a one-and-done kind of thing. You don't just start believing one day and it's all sunshine and rainbows from then on out. You have to continuously work to believe in yourself, and eventually you'll feel the difference. Because you become happier."

Maybe he's right, I think to myself, a small smile creeping onto my face as my parents open the door and come back inside from the deck.

"It was starting to get cold out there, but we wanted to give you your privacy, it looked like you guys were having a really deep conversation," my mom says.

"Yeah we were, and it actually was exactly what I needed to hear." I slowly exhale, as I feel the day melt away.

I Believe

The weekend slipped through our fingers as it does every week. Monday always comes around way too fast. In the dim morning light, I look through my closet for clothes to wear, fantasizing about the warmth lingering in the cozy sheets lining my bed and wishing I was still wrapped in them.

I finally settle on my favorite pair of jeans and a white sweater. Pulling them on, I walk into my bathroom in hopes of washing the sleepiness off my face. I turn the faucet on and hot water rushes down the drain. The steam wakes my senses.

Splashing the hot water onto my face, I rub the last bit of sleep out of my eyes. Looking up to pat my face dry, I look into the mirror to find Ethan standing behind me. I jump at the sight of him and scream a little louder than I should have. I mean, it is 6 o'clock in the morning!

"Ethan! Don't scare me like that!"

"Sorry," he laughs. "Anyway, I haven't been to good ole South Seattle High in a bit, so I thought it'd be fun to drive you to school today."

"Ethan, you literally graduated last year. The school looks exactly the same, what could you possibly have to reminisce on?"

"I don't know, I just feel so far removed from it all now since I don't go there every day anymore, you know."

"Yeah, I guess I get that. Anyway, I will take you up on that offer to drive me to school."

"Cool, but I get to choose the music we listen to."

"Are you implying my music is subpar?" I ask with a bit of sass. Ethan just shrugs with a sly smile, and I roll my eyes.

"Let me finish getting ready and grab some breakfast. Then we can go."

"Okay cool," Ethan says as he slinks slowly out of the bathroom throwing his hands into two thumbs up.

I run downstairs to grab two bananas and a granola bar from the pantry before throwing on my shoes and heading out the door. As soon as Ethan turns the car on, he plugs his phone in as fast as he can to ensure he gets to play his music. I turn and stare at him, shaking my head with a smile.

"Ethan, I said it was fine, you are allowed to play your music," I say chuckling a little bit.

"I know, force of habit. Back at school my teammates always fight over who gets to play their music and so it's always a race to see who can plugin first. I usually lose, so I think subconsciously I was wanting to win at a game we don't even play."

"You're ridiculous, let's just go to school," I laugh.

Ethan pulls up only two minutes before the first bell rings, before hopping out I look over at him.

"You're coming to my game tonight, right?"

"Wouldn't miss it."

I smile at him before shutting the door and waving as he drives away. Looking around I see the empty campus and realize I need to move my ass or I'll be late to English.

The day drags on slowly as nothing exciting happens. It's one of those Mondays that I tend to think created the whole "I hate Mondays" thing. Nevertheless, the school day comes to an end after I spend it incessantly watching the clock until it reads 2:25. The bell rings and I pack up my bag to head over to the locker room, where I find my entire team waiting for me.

"How did you guys get here so fast?" I ask with utter confusion.

"We ran," Addie says laughing, "Come on get dressed, it's go time!"

All of us change into our home uniforms of white shorts and emerald green jerseys, mine of course with 22 on the back. My lucky number. I start to lace up my cleats when my teammate Claudia starts to chant.

"I believe that we will win," the whole team echoes after her, "I believe that we will win. I believe that we will win. I believe that we will win!"

"Ow, ow, ow!" Claudia adds. It's her signature cheer that she cries out before and after every single game. I have played with her for two years now and it never gets old. It always makes me feel like we can take on the world before stepping onto the field.

With high spirits and even higher ponytails, we all file out of the locker room ready to start our pregame routine. We have an earlier game time than usual today, which is nice because we don't have much time to get nervous. Now, with an hour to warm up and get our game faces on, we are fired up. Coach John instructs us to get into three lines and start our drills as always, but he says to make sure that each person goes through each drill two times to ensure our touches are perfect.

We are playing the Seattle Heights Rangers today, one of the best teams in our league. So, we need our touches to be sharp and swift, and our passes crisp to beat them. After finishing drills, I feel confident.

"Let's finish up with some possession and shooting. All right, let's go!" Coach John yells with enthusiasm.

Filing into the box he created, we divide ourselves and play a game of rock, paper, scissors to see who gets to start with the ball. My team wins, and we hit it off with a bang. We complete our required five passes in no time at all and are switching the ball across the box effortlessly. My confidence skyrockets, and this time I am going to let it stay because I believe it is supposed to be there. Coach John tells us to cut possession short. We look good and he wants us to get some shots in before the game starts.

"Hey Coach, instead of our usual shooting drill, can we do two-on-two today?" I ask.

"All right Falcons, Hope has suggested we do two-on-two for our shooting drill and I think it's a great idea," Coach replies. "So, let's have the defenders line up into two lines, one on each side of the goal. Then the offense can line up in front of them on each side. Okay, let's do this!"

A few rounds into the drill and I have the ball on the left side of the field. I feel this desire to switch the ball across the field to hit Addie, who's running fiercely down the right-wing. I give in to it and switch the ball, watching it land perfectly a few feet in front of her as she runs to it and smashes it into the back of the goal. Coach, standing on the sideline watching us, starts clapping.

"Let's have Hope and Addie go to the call for captains. Nice work, everyone!" Addie and I run to the referee standing at half field with the captains from the Rangers. He tells us to shake hands, asking which side of the coin we want. Before I can say anything, Addie says, "Tails!"

He nods and tosses the coin into the air and we all watch intently as it cascades up toward the blinding sun and tumbles back down, landing beside our cleats tail side up. We have the first choice of what side of the field we want to start on, and we choose the side that puts the sun to our backs.

"All right Rangers, you will start with the ball. Falcons, you're on defense. Head back to your teams, get in formations, and be ready to start in two minutes!"

Less than two minutes later, we are lined up in our 4-4-3 formation and ready to go. Standing at the base of the circle at the midline, I eye the Ranger's forwards, who are shifting uncomfortably waiting for the whistle to blow. Seconds before the ref raises the whistle to his lips, I scan the bleachers looking for Ethan and find him in the front row beside my parents, and what looks like half of our school behind them.

The whistle blows directing my full attention to the game in front of me and my feet jump off the line, ready to take the ball from the forward charging toward me.

She tries to juke me out to the left but I've seen a simple juke like that a million times before, so I knew it was coming and mirror her shoulders as my feet work below me to steal the ball out from underneath her. The ball rolls right off her foot and onto mine as I start to charge down the middle of the field, with Addie on my right and Hailey on my left.

Looking ahead, I see a defender ready to block my path and quickly weave the ball from my left foot to my right and twist my body to face Addie as I pass the ball off to her unguarded. Addie takes the ball and speeds down the open alley to get into position to cross the ball over to either me or Hailey to finish. Addie pulls her right foot back and heaves it forward using all of her strength to force the ball toward me.

Watching as the ball arches toward my head, I jump up and nail it into the top right corner of the goal, scoring our first goal of the game. Making contact with the ground again, I race over to Addie to hug her.

"Yes! That was the perfect cross, Addie!"

"That header though, it was amazing! We are the dream team, let me just say."

Hustling back to our side of the field, I look into the bleachers once again to find Ethan up on his feet cheering me on. As I allow myself to relish in the glory of the goal I just scored, I also feel a streak of fear rising up. *Would I continue to believe in myself if I had missed that goal? Could I believe that I do create my own success?*

Despite my moments of self-doubt, we played great and the rest of the game went off without a hitch as we won 3-0, Addie and Claudia scoring the other two goals.

"What an amazing game, you guys!" I say to everyone, as we are in the locker room taking off our gear.

"Thanks to you for scoring that opening goal within minutes of the game starting and getting that momentum going for us!" Hailey responds.

"Oh stop it! You're making me blush," I say, getting a laugh out of my teammates. "But really you guys, we played so great tonight and I think we really do have a shot at winning the championship in two weeks."

"Me too," Addie agrees. "We will if we play with that same intensity. There is no doubt in my mind that we will take the trophy home." She pauses then gasps.

"Guys, I have an idea! Let's ask our parents if we can get ice cream to celebrate, and maybe Coach John will want to come too!"

"That would be so much fun!" I say and the whole team agrees it would be the best way to celebrate our victory.

Of course, our parents say yes. We laugh the entire drive to the ice cream shop talking about our favorite and funniest moments of the game. Like when Coach John jumped up and down when he realized there was no way for the Rangers to catch up and that we were going to win.

As we sit around a large round table I look around at my teammates and find myself feeling so happy and proud of them. While I may not fully believe in myself, I sure as hell believe that this team is destined for greatness.

Just Boring

Riding high from our incredible win last night, I stroll into English class with a huge smile on my face and my head high. I see the usual suspects, my classmate Avery who is always nice to me, my classmate Brody who I also have had a massive crush on since 8th grade, and my former best friend Katie, who just so happens to be Brody's girlfriend.

Katie, of course, looks absolutely nothing like me. She has blonde hair, bright blue eyes, sweet little freckles on her heart-shaped face, and legs for days. Did I mention she is 5'9"? I on the other hand am 5'2" with dark brown curly hair, hazel eyes that I got from my mom, and dark brown hair all over my arms, thanks to my dad. So, I know I have no chance of ever attracting Brody's attention, but I can hope he at least wants to be friends. Over the years, we have talked some and have had a few classes together here and there, but ever since Katie started dating him last year, I knew any sort of shot I had was blown.

It really hurt that she went for him knowing that I have had a crush on him for forever, but I mean we weren't friends anymore anyway. I guess I can't really blame her, but it still stung. I had almost wanted to say something to her about it and let her know that my feelings were hurt, but I thought better of it because she probably wouldn't have given me the time of day anyway.

It didn't always used to be like that though. We used to be like sisters, we were inseparable. We met in elementary school playing on the same soccer team. I remember seeing her for the first time and thinking that she had the coolest hair. I had never seen someone's hair so naturally blonde that it was almost white. And being the bubbly seven-year-old that I was, I told her how cool I thought it was. From then on, we talked about everything and anything, and were always together.

But that all changed the summer after eighth grade. We said our tearful goodbyes before Katie left to spend the summer in France with her cousins and grandparents who live there. I had spent the summer playing in different soccer tournaments across the country. We knew communicating would be difficult with the time difference. When I was going to sleep, she was waking up. I had still hoped we would make it work, but we didn't talk that entire summer. It had been the longest amount of time we had ever gone without speaking, and it didn't just change our friendship. It ended it.

When Katie returned from Europe, she looked and acted like a different person. She had grown at least four inches, her hair was longer, her body slimmer, and her boobs seemed to have grown at least two cup sizes. While my boobs had felt like they had shrunk, my height hadn't budged since sixth grade, and my hair was just as curly and frustrating as it had always been.

I had been excited to ask about her trip and the amazing sights, but when I called she told me she didn't want to be friends anymore. She had said that she was ready for a fresh start in high school and felt like we needed to meet new people. Once school started she became unbelievably popular, while I floated from group to group as I looked for another friend who understood me the way Katie used to. Had I done something wrong? Was there something wrong with me?

These questions continue to rattle around my brain like marbles in a tin can, making so much noise I still can't decipher which thoughts are true and which are coming from fear of not being good enough. It's now our junior year and I still haven't found a friend like Katie had been.

So now as I sit at my desk two seats away from Brody and across the room from Katie, I try to put our past out of my mind and focus on my teacher giving a lecture about *Macbeth*. Ugh, Shakespeare just doesn't make sense to me. I try so hard to understand Elizabethan English, but the words seem made-up. It all looks like gibberish to me.

After finishing her lecture, Mrs. Gray pairs us into groups to work on posters to help us better understand the material. To my surprise, I get paired with Brody and Avery. We look at each other, listen to the noise of the classroom getting increasingly louder, and decide it's probably best if we go and work out in the hall.

After we get settled, Avery suggests we divvy up the work between the three of us and volunteers to take plot structure. Brody takes the theme. I am left with explaining why the choice of diction and tone matter. Great, I think, and try to hide my dissatisfaction with my portion of the work, but Brody catches on.

"Hope, we can switch if you want."

"Oh no, it's okay. I should stick with this anyway, it'll be a good challenge."

"Challenge? You're like super smart, you'll breeze through this!" Here we go again, if only I truly believed that.

"Thanks Brody, but for some reason, Shakespeare just goes in one ear and out the other for me. I just don't get it."

"Tell me about it. It doesn't make any sense, I have to re-read the lines over and over again just to sort of understand what he is trying to say."

"I know, right? I swear I have sat here just staring at the page because I have re-read the same line at least ten times and still don't understand," I say laughing.

"You are literally describing me last night when I was scrambling to finish our assigned reading. I just sat on the floor in my room so confused about something I 'read' a few lines ago that I couldn't even focus on the words I was trying to read at that moment," he says as pink circles form on his cheeks, surrounding his light brown freckles. He looks away and laughs.

"Hey guys, I hate to break up your little moment but we only have twenty minutes to finish this thing before class is over," Avery interjects.

"Yeah, you're right, Avery," Brody smiles again. "We don't want Mrs. Gray coming over and yelling at us for wasting time."

"Right, the poster. We definitely should be focusing on this right now," I say, blushing in deeper shades of pink and red than Brody.

We bury our heads into our work and finish with three minutes to spare. Thanks to Avery helping me out a little bit, my interpretation of language and tone came out pretty good.

Walking back into the classroom to hand our poster off to Mrs. Gray, I catch Katie's eye as lines crease her forehead and a frown forms on her lips. I give the poster to Mrs. Gray and walk back to my seat to pack up my things as quickly as I can to get the hell out of here. Who knows what Katie has to say to me, and I know that I don't really want to hear it based on how angry she looks. The bell rings and I am the first one out the door. But my escape doesn't go to plan as Katie steps in front of me, stopping me in my tracks.

"Listen, Hope. The entire class could hear you and Brody laughing and talking like it was nobody's business. I am not going to stop you from being friends, but if you think for a second that you could take him from me you are wrong and will regret it," Katie says with a smirk.

"Katie, I would never do that, that is not the kind of person I am. But hey, maybe your idea of the person I am is warped. I still don't understand why you decided that person wasn't good enough to be your friend anymore."

"Jesus, Hope. Are you really going to do this right now?"

"Yeah, actually. Now is as good a time as ever because every other time I have tried to bring this up, you dodge it. So just tell me, why did you ditch me?"

"Fine, do you really want to know?"

"Yes, that's why I am asking."

"You're just, boring," she sighs.

"Your words don't bring anything interesting to the table and neither do your looks, so yeah," she continues. "And I mean if I'm being honest, it seems like everybody else at school agrees with me because you don't seem to have any friends."

Me or Her

I stare at Katie, the blankness coats my face like paint on a wall that conceals the nail holes and dents beneath.

"Sorry Hope, it's the truth. Listen I got to go, my friends are waiting for me," she forces a laugh that sounds so insincere I start to wonder if she really meant what she said.

A tear begins to roll down my cheek. Wiping my eye, I rush to the bathroom in hopes that no one saw what just went down. As soon as I walk through the door I begin checking to make sure no one is in one of the stalls. Looking at myself in the fingerprint-covered mirror, I see my reddened face interlaced with dark shadows from the bright white lights above and I find myself in my head again.

I can't believe that someone I used to share everything with... my secrets, my fears, my wildest dreams... just treated me like all of that meant nothing to her. Like I was nothing to her.

Lost in my thoughts, I am startled by the bathroom door slowly creaking open and Avery's face appearing in the mirror beside me.

"Hey. I saw what happened out there, don't worry I think I was the only one, but I just wanted to check in and see how you're doing."

"Thanks Avery, umm I'm not doing great," I force a laugh.

"I don't think anyone would be after having someone talk to them like that. But listen, as hard as it might be right now I want you to understand something my mom told me when I was younger," she whispers, as she glances over at the stall doors.

"She told me that sometimes when people say hurtful things to you, it may have absolutely nothing to do with you and everything to do with them," she continues as she looks back at me.

"We have no idea what other people are thinking or feeling inside when they speak to us, whether their words are kind or unkind," she smiles. "So, it's important to try and not take everything people say so seriously, even if what they are saying is fueled with the intention of hurting us. I don't know Katie very well and so I can't speak to what she might be going through in her life, but I know that you are not boring."

"Thank you, Avery, that means a lot," I smile back. "And your mom sounds like a wise woman."

"And I hate to spread rumors but I feel like it might be appropriate here," Avery shrugs as she quickly reapplies her lip gloss in the mirror. "I heard that Katie's parents are getting a divorce, so maybe that played a role in why she spoke to you the way she did."

"Wow, I had no idea. I hope that rumor isn't true," I find myself saying.

"I know this is getting heavy, but do you want to get some lunch?" Avery turns to look at me again.

"I'd love to."

As we walk to the lunchroom I think more about what Avery said. I may or may not be boring in Katie's eyes, but what she thinks or says about me might really have more to do with her than it does me.

Thunderstorms

As I walk out of the lunchroom with Avery on the way to biology class, I look up and notice that the clouds are unusually dark and the sun is nowhere to be seen.

"Avery, look at how dark the clouds are. They almost look black," I say.

"Oh, yeah. Whoa, those look like thunderstorm clouds to me."

"I hope they aren't, we need every practice we can get if we want to make it to the championship."

"Do they cancel practice for thunderstorms? I mean a little rain never hurt anybody. We do live in Seattle."

"I know, but if there's lightning then they have to cancel because the field is surrounded by metal bleachers." As if on cue, it starts pouring and lightning surges through the sky, emanating blue and purple light in all directions. Nothing at all like the typical Seattle drizzle.

"Great," I add, "let's go before we get struck."

We run through the rain as fast as we can in hopes of not getting too wet, but by the time we get to class we are soaked through. This is going to be a really fun class, I think to myself as I slink down into my seat.

A few hours later the bell dismisses us for the day and I walk outside to find that it is still pouring, and thunder is still clapping against the ominous clouds.

"Practice is canceled, right?" I text Addie.

"Yep, I just talked to Coach and he said there is no way we will be able to practice in this weather safely," she texts back.

"Ugh, bummer. I guess there is always tomorrow, but I was really looking forward to practice today."

"Me too."

I put my phone in my back pocket and run toward my car, holding my backpack over my head for cover. Rushing to open my car door, I trip and my backpack slips right out of my hands and drops to the ground. Great, I think to myself as I collect my backpack off of the ground, shaking it wildly to get as much water off as possible.

Throwing my bag into the passenger seat, I start the car and feel the raindrops dangling from my clothing glide down my arms and legs, staining the leather seats. This is going to be a very uncomfortable drive home. Looking out and into the miserable sky, I reflect on the equally miserable feeling I experienced earlier. The nasty words that came out of Katie's mouth sting all over again, while the words of encouragement from Avery fade into the background like the sun behind the clouds.

You're just boring.

But it isn't her words that cause the most pain, it's that they validate the same thoughts I have about myself on my worst days. The same thoughts that I try and stuff deep into an emotional vault in hopes that they won't escape. She said everything I fear most about myself. And maybe she's right. Maybe other people think what I think too. My looks aren't interesting, my curly hair is too much, my muscular thighs are too big, and my short figure isn't attractive. Maybe Katie is right.

I shake my head and direct my focus to the road in front of me, in hopes of escaping the tidal wave of emotion trying to pull me under. But it doesn't last very long because as I pull into my driveway I no longer have the energy to stop the tears.

Hot tears flow onto my cheeks, like the rain falling and flooding my windshield. My chest heaves as I gasp for air between sobs, just letting the sadness overcome me because I can't outrun it anymore. I hold myself as I start to shiver from the cold rain that is still seeping into my clothes, and from the realization that the kind words of motivation and understanding from friends and family won't mean anything until I truly and fully believe them myself.

Until I stop thinking only maybe they're right, or maybe I'm enough, none of it matters. Gathering my things I go inside, and to my surprise no one is around to greet me so I head upstairs to my room. I push open the door only to run straight into my mom sorting laundry.

"Hey Hope, how was your day?"

"Fine."

"That doesn't sound promising," she looks up. "Oh, Hope what's wrong?"

"Just a tough day at school that's all, I'll be okay," I say, trying to hold it together.

"I don't want to push, but I think it might help if we talk about it."

"You're probably right, it's just kind of heavy and I don't want to unload on you because I am sure you have plenty of other things to do and worry about."

"Hope, nothing is more important to me right now than listening to how you feel. I want to hear it."

"Okay, well at least let me change out of my wet clothes."

Getting into my comfiest pair of sweats and my softest sweatshirt, I meet my mom on my bed and prepare to share everything that's on my mind and everything that I have kept inside for so long.

"So, what's up, Hope?" she asks.

"A lot of things, and I guess today really amplified them. Before I start though, can I ask you something?"

"Sure," she answers.

"Have you ever felt like no matter what you do it will never be enough? Like it doesn't matter if you put your heart and soul into it, it just doesn't seem good enough, it doesn't seem like anybody will care?"

"What are you referring to?"

"Nothing in particular, honestly. I guess I'm referring to everything, even thinking back to our game the other day. Like I know that I played well, I scored the opening goal and afterward I was feeling really good about myself, but now that I am thinking back on it I could've done so much more. My passes could've been crisper, my touches could've been cleaner, and I could've made more of an effort to congratulate everyone after the game."

"Why all of a sudden are you obsessing over all of this? It seems like you have been in such high spirits the past few days?"

"I don't know. I guess today just reminded me of everything that brings me down, everything that makes me feel like I am not enough. Old thoughts bubbled to the surface and old friends destroyed my confidence."

"Well, tell me about today. I'm here to listen."

"I mean it started out great, I was feeling really good about our first playoff win and I was excited to go to English. Which you know is my favorite class, so I was in a good mood. Mrs. Gray was talking about Shakespeare and she assigned a project that we had to finish by the end of class and paired us up into groups to complete it. I got paired up with Avery and Brody."

"Isn't Brody the cute one you've had a thing for the past little while?" my mom interrupts.

"Yes," I answer slowly, "Anyway, I was joking with him about how we don't really understand Shakespeare all that well, and that the language is just so hard to make sense of, and I guess Katie heard us laughing together."

"I haven't heard you mention her name in a while. I didn't realize she's in one of your classes."

"Yeah, well there is a reason for that, and what made this situation so bad is that she is Brody's girlfriend. So, as we finished up our project and we went to turn it in, I caught Katie's eye and could tell she was pissed. I tried to rush out of the room once class was over, but she caught up to me and just unleashed on me."

"What did she say?"

"She basically accused me of trying to steal her boyfriend, which I would never do. So I asked why she'd think I would do that because she should know I am not that type of person. But then I thought, maybe her idea of who I am is something really horrible. Why else would she have cut ties with me so abruptly all those years ago? So, I asked her that too, I asked her what made her think that I was no longer good enough to be friends with and what makes her think I would try to take something from her. And she gave me an answer that I was not expecting to hear."

"Oh jeez, I do not miss high school. What did she say to you?"

"She told me that her reasoning for abandoning our friendship was that I am boring and that what I have to say and what I look like is not interesting to her. And apparently to the rest of the school too, because she pointed out the fact that I don't have many friends," I say the last part a bit shaky.

"Hope, that is horrible. I am so sorry."

"The thing is, on my worst days I actually believe that I am not interesting or pretty enough to be desired by a friend or a boy. I believe that I don't have what It takes to be good enough at soccer or in school. And I believe that I am not enough just as I am because I think I am boring, uninteresting and ugly."

"Hope," my mom says, tears glistening in her hazel eyes, "I had no idea you felt like that, I should've paid more attention. I am so sorry."

"It's okay Mom, I am pretty good at keeping things bottled up inside, so I wouldn't have expected you to know," I say, keeping my head low so I don't have to look into her eyes and see pity. "Avery told me today that she heard a rumor that Katie's parents are getting a divorce. I remember how close Katie always was with her parents, and so if that rumor is true, it must be really hard for her."

"Yeah. That doesn't mean her words don't hurt by any means, but it makes you think that maybe she is hurting too."

"Yeah," I say as I look up, meeting my mom's face, looking soft in the warm light of the bedroom. Feeling vulnerable and unprotected I say, "You know, I don't really feel like talking about this anymore. I'm sorry."

"Don't be sorry, I will give you some space. I love you so much," she says as he hugs me.

"I love you too, Mom." I watch as she leaves my room, closing the door softly behind her and I start to wonder, why is it so hard for me to believe in myself?

What reason do I have to believe that I am not good enough? Why is it so hard for me to take the positive things my friends and family have to say to me as truth?

The questions circle 'round and 'round in my mind, and I search for the answers but they are nowhere to be found.

The Big Day

Two weeks have come and gone since I broke down crying after my run-in with Katie. In those two weeks, my soccer team and I have won each and every one of our playoff games. Ethan went back to college, and my mindset is more or less the same.

Despite my achievements and all the great things happening around me, I still feel like I will never measure up to the idea of who I am supposed to be in my head. But I am desperately trying to push my thoughts in a positive direction because today is the big day. It's the day of the championship game. I can and can't believe that we made it here, but now that we are here I am so ready to see what we can do!

Addie and I have been talking about the game all day during class, passing periods, pretty much any chance we can get. We're playing our long-time rivals, the Eagles from North Seattle High School. We almost lost to them in our playoff game last week but pulled through and scored two goals in the last three minutes of the game. So, today we have got to stay on our toes.

The school day drags on slowly, and when the bell finally rings we are ready to put our uniforms on, lace up our cleats, and kick some Eagle ass. Excited to get changed and ready to go, I literally run to the locker room, nearly tripping over myself. I fling the locker room door open to find all of my teammates already inside, waiting for me.

"How am I always the last one here? I literally ran all the way here. Scratch that, I sprinted!" I say, still out of breath.

"Maybe it's those short little legs of yours. They just can't get you where you need to go fast enough," Addie laughs, and the rest of the team joins in good fun.

"Oh shut up," I laugh. "My little legs can outrun you any day."

"Mm-hmm, okay," Addie says playfully.

"It's okay, you're doing your best. You can't help that you are so short," I pat my legs lovingly and get a good laugh out of the team.

"You are ridiculous," Claudia says, shaking her head laughing. "Let's just get changed because we have a championship to win!"

After we all get changed, throw our hair up into ponytails, and lace up our cleats, Claudia chants her "I believe" and "ow, ow, ow." Before we know it, it's game time. Nerves begin to rise up from my toes, tingling their way into my stomach, creating that butterfly sensation I always get before games.

Concentrating on the mounting tornado of swirling butterflies in my stomach, I almost miss the referee calling for captains, but Addie grabs my arm and we race over eager to claim our side of the field.

"Okay Lady Falcons, heads or tails?"

"Heads," I say.

"All right, Eagles. You are tails. Now, I'm going to flip this coin and whoever's side lands face up gets to choose which side of the field they want to start on. Okay?"

"Got it," we all say in unison. He flips the coin, launching it high up into the air and as it falls, flipping over itself, I pray it will land heads up. My prayer didn't quite work as I hoped because the coin lands tails side up and the Eagles choose to start on the right side of the field.

"Okay, Eagles you will start with the ball and Falcons you will be on the defense. Go back to your teams and get into formation because the game will start in three minutes."

We run back to our teammates and coach to give them the low down and Coach starts us off in our signature 4-4-3 formation, with Addie, Claudia, Hailey, and I lined up along the midline. I wait nervously as the ref draws the whistle to his lips, the fact that we are playing for the state title sets in and the nerves rev up. He finally blows the whistle and we're off, the ball quickly bounces from player to player as the Eagles try and weave through our defense.

Their star player, number 39, takes the ball with force and I call for Addie to switch positions with me because I think I will have the better angle in taking her on. As she charges forward I square off to her right hip and prepare to defend her with all that I have.

She moves the ball effortlessly between her two feet, touching the ball lightly but with intention, and I realize if I don't make a move now she will most likely blow past me and score a goal, which I do not want. So, I watch as she fakes to the right, keeping my shoulders square to the field in front of me and as her body comes back through the center I lunge at her right foot carrying the ball and I take it in stride.

I force the ball forward with power and sprint down the field faster than I ever have before. Looking to my left and right, I find Addie and my other teammate Rose on either side to support me and I know what I need to do. I start to fake a pass over to Addie, but right before my foot makes contact with the ball I contort my body to face Rose and drive my leg through the ball creating a perfect pass landing right at her feet.

Rose pushes the ball forward, swiftly weaving in and out of their defense, moving closer and closer to the goal. Seeing how close she is to the goal and how close we are to putting our first point up on the scoreboard, I yell out to her, "Rose! Shoot now!"

She swings her leg back and shoves it forward into the ball, driving it straight into the back of the net. The goalie didn't even stand a chance. I run over to her with the biggest smile spread across my face,

"There you go, Rose!"

"Thanks, Hope! Now let's get another one!"

"That's what I like to hear, let's do it."

As we set up again behind the center circle waiting for the Eagles to kick-off, a cool confidence settles on our shoulders and a fire lights up in our eyes.

In what seems like minutes later, the sharp and shrill sound of the referee's whistle signals for half-time, and Coach John calls us over to the sideline.

"Okay, we are up 2-1, thanks to Rose's goal in the first part of the half and Hailey's goal just a few minutes ago. But, we need to keep in mind that the Eagles are not going to let up just because we have the upper hand right now. So, we need to keep the intensity up and play like the amazing soccer players that I know you guys are. Okay?"

"Okay," we all say with determination surging through our faces.

"All right, Falcons on three. 1, 2, 3!"

"Falcons!"

With a burst of energy and confidence, we run back onto the field, ready to take on whatever is thrown our way. Because the Eagles started with the ball in the first half, we have kick-off and Addie motions for me to take it. Stepping up to the midline, I eye my opponents with a surprising sheer conviction and confidence that I will get the ball past their defense and into their goal. I wait patiently for the whistle to blow granting me the permission to start the second half of the game with a bang.

The piercing high pitched sound rings in my ear, as I turn to pass the ball to Claudia standing behind me. She takes the ball and signals for me to cross the field and run down the right sideline. I sprint into position and call for the ball hoping she can get it to me before a defender steps in to defend me.

Luckily, she switches the ball across the field just in time, as I am able to take the ball down from the air and swiftly maneuver around the defender charging toward me. I race down the wide-open alley and look for a teammate to pass to since I don't have the right angle to take a shot right now. Addie shoots her hands up calling out to me,

"Hope, I'm open!"

I cross the ball over to her and make a run for the right goalpost, to support her on the off chance she misses the goal. Addie runs forward dodging her defender and shoots the ball directly at me.

Knowing that the ball will hit the goalpost if I don't do something, I jump up as high as I can and ram my head into the side of the ball powering it into the left side of the net, watching as the ball grazes through the goalie's gloves and into the goal.

"Yes!" I scream as a rush of confidence washes over me. Addie sprints over to me squeezing me into the tightest hug I think I have ever gotten.

"Addie, I love you, but I...can't...breathe," I say gasping for air.

"Sorry, I'm just so excited, that was amazing!"

"Thanks, Addie!"

"Come on, let's go celebrate with the rest of our team," she says as she starts to run back to our side of the field.

Following suit I start running, but all of a sudden a sharp pain shoots through my right knee. I tell myself it's probably no big deal and nothing to worry about. But as I make my way back to my position behind the center circle the pain only increases, and a thought that I have feared most throughout my entire soccer career flashes through my head. What if this pain is the precursor to an ACL tear?

My heart stops for a moment as I reel from that terrifying thought. As hard as I try to shove it out of my mind, I can't seem to shake it and the fear mounts. Should I tell someone? No, I should just try and play through it. It's probably nothing. But what if it isn't?

A shiver runs down my spine as the whistle is blown, signaling for the Eagles to take the kick-off.

I try to turn my focus back to the game in front of me but it keeps circling back to the daunting idea of an injury. Lost in my thoughts I don't see my opponent charging at me, and before I can even try and prepare to defend her, she runs right into me and sends my body through the air.

All I can do is wait to hit the ground and pray that I don't land on my right side, but as I am approaching the ground I realize my right knee is aimed straight at the ground and I land right on it. And resembling the catchphrase of Rice Krispie cereal my knee goes, snap, crackle, pop, and I already know my worst fear just became my reality. I just tore my ACL.

I scream out crying, writhing around on the ground in immense pain. Coach John comes running over to me and asks what happened and all I can say is that I am sorry.

"Why are you sorry? Don't be sorry, injuries happen. It's okay!"

"I just don't want to let the team down, I want to keep playing," I say in between breathless sobs.

"You are not letting anyone down, you have my word on that. Okay? Now, what happened?"

"I think I tore my ACL, I heard a popping noise and I can't move my knee."

"All right, let me carry you to the sidelines and we will get everything figured out."

As Coach lifts me into his arms, and my teammates, opponents, and crowd cheer for me and recovery, all I can think about is how lifeless my leg feels dangling from my hip and cascading over Coach's arm. I start to feel woozy and as I look up at the sky above me, my eyes start to close and my consciousness fades and everything turns into a deep dark black.

Simply Enough

My eyes feel heavy as I struggle to open them, but when I finally get them open the bright white lights of the hospital room flood in, and I am reminded of the events of the game. I look over to find my mom sitting beside me with hopeful eyes and a soft smile brightening her tired face.

"Hey sweetheart, how are you feeling?"

"Okay. I'm not in too much pain so that's good." My gaze wanders down toward my right leg and my eyes go wide. "Did I get surgery?"

"Yes, you did. I know that cast is kind of an eyesore. Usually it takes a few weeks to get in for an ACL repair, but you got lucky and a very nice man named Dr. Jones was on call and willing to operate."

"Oh. Well, that's good I guess. Sorry, this is just a lot to process."

"It's okay, no need to be sorry, I don't even know what I would be thinking right now if I were in your shoes."

"Thanks, Mom. Oh, what was the result of the game? Did my teammates pull through? Are we state champs?" My mom breathes out slowly and looks down.

"I'm sorry honey, they tried. They really tried their best but everyone was in shock and scared for you. So, unfortunately, the Eages took the title, 4-3."

My face falls and my chest feels heavy, I can't help but feel sad for myself and my teammates. We worked so hard to get to the championship and because of me, we lost. Before I can get too caught up in the idea that my injury cost the team the championship, the door of my hospital room suddenly bursts open and a man I assume is Dr. Jones walks in accompanied by two nurses.

"Hey there, Hope. I just wanted to come in and check on you to see how you were doing, and also to let you know that you will be discharged in a couple of hours to go home and rest."

"Hi, Dr. Jones. Umm, I am doing okay. I am in a little bit of pain but it's nothing I can't handle. So, I'm doing fine."

"Good, good. Okay, well I am just going to take your mom outside for a minute to talk to her about your recovery process and the extent of the injury, okay?"

"Okay, thank you for coming to check on me."

"Of course."

"Hope, I'll be back in a little bit," my mom says as she squeezes my hand lovingly. As everyone files out of the room and the door closes, I look out the window of the room and lose myself in my thoughts.

Hours pass and before I know it I am sitting in the backseat of my mom's car watching as we travel down the path I have traveled a million times before. The path home. Pulling into our driveway, my mom shuts off the car and quickly gets out to help me walk up to the house. I prop open the car door with my crutch and try to slide my way down to the ground, but my cast gets caught on the lip of the bottom of the car and I fall hard and fast to the ground.

"Hope, are you okay? Here let me help you up."

"No! I just want to do this myself, please," I say as I grit my teeth in pain.

"Okay, I'm here if you need me."

I push myself up on my crutches and use my left leg to stand all the way up, and as my eyes meet my mom's, tears begin to blur my vision and I just can't hold it in anymore.

"Oh honey, come here," my mom says, wrapping her arms around me, holding me steady in a secure hug.

"Mom I can't do this," I say gasping for air, "I mean, just yesterday I was running up and down the soccer field, playing in the state championship and now I can't even get out of the car without falling flat on my face."

"Hope, you just had a major surgery and your body is not ready to be back on the soccer field right now. This is where you are at and that has to be okay for now. You will get there again, I promise you. Let's go inside and get you situated in your room so you can rest, okay?"

"Okay," I say as I slowly follow her up the driveway and into the house, hobbling on my crutches.

I get up to my bed and stare down at my cast before I start to cry all over again, and my mom tries to comfort me.

"Hope, it's going to be okay, this is just part of your journey and it's not going to be forever."

"I know, but it's stopping me from doing the things that I love and even from doing everyday normal things like getting out of the car or walking up the stairs by myself. I just feel like I can't do anything anymore."

"Well, that is just not true.'

"It feels like it though,' I say sniffling. "I mean the past few weeks have been so hard. Do you remember the day that I came home from school and walked into my room crying while you were sorting my laundry?"

"Yes, very well, and I remember what Katie said to you. It was so awful."

"Yeah, it was. And now that I am here with a huge cast hindering me from everything I am overwhelmed with that same feeling I felt after having that conversation with Katie. In every sense of the word I just don't feel good enough," I say, this time huge heaving sobs come out of me and I don't even try to stop them. My mom looks at me with warmth and love in her eyes.

"Hope you are good enough, there is absolutely no doubt in my mind that you are good enough and that you are worthy. You are incredible, whether you choose to believe that or not. And I just want to tell you that I am proud of you, because despite feeling like you aren't capable and that you aren't enough you have achieved so much."

"You helped to lead your soccer team to the state championship," she continues. "You are doing your best in school, and your best is pretty damn good. And, you are the kindest sister and the most thoughtful daughter. So, even though I don't know what it feels like to walk a day in your shoes, just know that I hear you. And on the days that you don't believe that you are worthy or enough, just know that I do. I believe in you and love you beyond measure."

Her words were what I have needed and longed to hear for so long, and now I don't even know what to say. But knowing that she sees me and she sees somebody whose presence is meaningful, is everything and more. I fall into her open arms and just sit in her embrace as tears silently stream down my face, feeling in every sense of the word "seen."

"Oh sweetheart, did I say something wrong?"

"No. No, you said everything right, thank you, I really needed to hear that," I say smiling, wiping my tears, "I just feel this pressure to be perfect and to do things in a way that will ensure that whatever I'm doing is enough. Like I have to plan things out super deliberately and study twice over to lessen the rate of mistakes I might make. I like to feel like I am winning or succeeding at something, to distract myself from the fear that I'm not worthy of anything else. I'm not worthy of taking a break, or even of truly believing in myself. Like during our playoff game that Ethan came to, I don't think I even wanted to admit this to myself but I had to score that opening goal to feel like my 'belief' in myself was warranted because I felt like if my belief system didn't produce a result than it was for nothing. And I know that sounds crazy, but honestly, that is what goes through my head most days and I don't know how to make it stop."

"Hope, I wish I knew what to say to make you feel better, but I have no idea what to say other than I love you. I believe in you, and I know that that doesn't take away any of the pain you are feeling."

"It's okay, Mom. I don't know what to say either. I have been trying to find the words through the advice of others for a while now and still haven't found the right ones that completely inspire me to change the way I think about and see myself."

My mom's eyes light up and she stands to grab an envelope from my desk.

"Maybe those words will come when you least expect it and from who you least expect," she said as she handed me a letter. "This was dropped off for you at the hospital and I think now is as good a time as ever to give it to you. Read it and you'll see that more people believe in you than you know."

I take the envelope from her hand and see that it is addressed to me from school. Unsure of its contents, I open it warily because usually when you get a letter from school it's not always good news. Taking the letter out of the envelope, I see a detailed paragraph written on the front signed by my principal and soccer coach. Confused and intrigued I start to read.

Dear Hope,

We have been so inspired by your bravery and determination to help lead your team to the state championship, and even more so by the grit you displayed in the game yesterday. The fact that you contracted a severe injury during the game and still wanted to play to support your team shows that you are an excellent leader and care a lot about the people around you. We value those traits very highly and we are so proud that you are a part of the South Seattle High School community.

With that being said, we want to ask you to come back to school whenever you are ready and give a speech about your experience on the soccer team, during and after the championship. We believe that your incredible leadership as co-captain this past season will allow you to construct a speech that is inspiring and all-encompassing of the amazing things you and your teammates have accomplished this year. It would be wonderful to hear about how you and your teammates worked together to make it to the championship and about what challenges you experienced along the way. We hope you give our proposal some consideration as we know the entire student body would love to hear what you have to say. We wish you a quick and smooth recovery and hope you can come back to school and join us all very soon.

Warmest regards,
Principal Adams and Coach John

I am not even sure what I was expecting to read when I opened that letter, but it definitely wasn't that.

"So, now do you see what I am trying to get you to see? So many people see so much good in you and they all believe in you. You are the only person in your way and you deserve to believe in yourself as much as everyone else does. You are worthy of love and care, you are worthy of celebration and success, and you are more than good enough if I haven't said that already."

And whether it was my mom's words or the heat of the moment, I may never know, but for some reason I have no desire to keep tearing myself down for not winning the game my teammates and I worked so hard to qualify for. I have no desire to fuel the thought that because I tore my ACL we didn't win. This lack of desire to tear myself down surges past the result of the game, and I also no longer have the desire to curse myself for the body that I do or do not have. And I no longer have the desire to fit perfectly into this arbitrary idea of who I am supposed to be in my head. My only desire is to capture these epiphanies in writing so that I never forget this moment, the moment where I am letting everything be as it is.

A smile comes to my face as I say, "Hey Mom, can I have a piece of paper and a pen?"

"Absolutely, and actually better yet, you can have your journal. Whatever shift just happened, write all about it because that smile looks good on you."

She hands me my journal and I flip to the first blank page and I start writing, my thoughts become words on paper, they just flow out of me.

"The life of a girl in the 21st century is a battle, a battle that unless you are facing it you won't truly understand. As I've grown up I've watched commercials where women pinch and prod at these things called 'imperfections' or 'flaws,' and I watched as beauty and cosmetic companies created products that were said to magically cure something that never needed fixing to begin with. On Disney Channel I watched princesses and my favorite characters, who all without fail had the same body type, thin, small waist, big boobs, and a big booty, waltz around getting guy after guy.

Yet, when Cinderella came around and she didn't wear makeup or have tight clothing to accentuate her body she wasn't deemed beautiful. It was only when she had a fairy godmother to cast a spell granting her the perfect dress and hairdo to create the ideal image, one that we are all made to believe is the epitome of beauty, was she deemed worthy. It was only then that she got the guy, and when the spell started to wear off she ran away in fear that nobody would like her without all the props, nobody would think she was beautiful just as she was. I remember thinking Cinderella was so lucky to have someone to make her look appealing to everyone and anyone with the flick of a wand.

As I grew older and the princesses of Disney began to bore me and the excitement of social media started to intrigue me, the pressure to be perfect came creeping in from every angle. The pressure to be the perfect straight-A student who never fails, to be an all-star soccer player because if I didn't make varsity I wasn't good at my sport, and the pressure to achieve that ideal body type I had watched on TV my whole life. It just feels like the world is yelling at me in every capacity possible that I am not good enough. I'm not pretty enough. I'm not smart enough. And I'm not successful enough.

When can enough just be enough? Why can't the muscular arms and legs that allow me to play soccer be enough? Why can't the extra fat on my waistline that protects my vital organs be enough? Why can't the 92 on the math test I worked my ass off for be enough? When will I be enough? I'm so tired of trying to be this perfect person all the time who strives to win at every game put in front of her... the best soccer player, the best student, the best daughter, the best sister, and the best friend.

The more I try to win and push myself to be perfect, the worse I feel about myself because even if I succeed I never feel like it is enough. I'm so tired of believing that I am not enough. I don't want to be that perfect person all the time. I make mistakes. I deal with anxiety and depression and am not happy all the time like I am told to be. I don't have the perfect body type and honestly I probably never will unless I kill myself for it, and I never want to put myself through that. So, I'm done. I'm done giving in to the pressure of trying to be good enough for somebody else's standards. I'm done trying to be perfect because perfect is overrated anyway. I am enough, simply because I am."

Tears stream down my face and a smile rests on my lips as I set my pen down beside me. My mom sees the tears.

"Oh Hope, are you all right?"

"Yeah, actually I am," I say, the smile on my face widening, "I just wrote the most empowering journal entry and made a promise to myself that I am really proud of."

"Hope, that is wonderful, I am so happy for you." Now my mom's face is streaming with tears,

"Thanks, Mom. I'm happy for me too, because promising to let myself be enough simply because I am feels really, really good."

The Most Fulfilling Thing

It has been two weeks since my surgery and a week since I made my sacred promise to myself, to trust that I am enough simply because I am. I haven't gone back to school yet but my teammates and some of my classmates have come over to the house to drop off gifts of ice cream, flowers, and "get well soon" cards.

Despite laying in bed, being in pain, and not being able to move my right leg much at all, I have felt so loved these past few weeks and ironically I feel the most confident I have ever felt in my life. I feel this sense of belonging in the world now because I realized that the world has had a spot for me all along. It was just waiting for me to see that I don't need to change anything about myself, my appearance, or my values to slide right into it. I just needed to start believing that I am enough just as I am. I wish that I was able to see that sooner, but of course I had to walk through the darkness to recognize that truth and reach this bright light.

It's weird, because in the past whenever I started to feel better I expected the bad days to just disappear. But now I feel like I will be okay even if those bad days come, even if those uncomfortable emotions rise up within me, because I know that rain has to fall to water the flowers of growth. I smile as I think about that and I sink deeper into the comforts of my bed, snuggling in with the pillow my parents bought me since they know most of my recovery consists of lots of rest. I didn't realize how tired I was, and am surprised as my eyes flutter downwards, closing softly. As I drift off to sleep, the sound of my door creaking open startles me, and I look over towards it and find my mom standing there with the letter from school in her hand.

"Hey Hope, how are you doing?"

"I'm good, still in a little bit of pain, but I took some ibuprofen like an hour ago, so that's been helping."

"Good, so its been a few weeks. Have you given any thought to whether or not you want to give that speech your principal and coach talked about?"

"Yeah, I have and I decided I want to do it."

My mom smiles, "So, how do you think you want your speech to play out?"

"Well, they were wanting me to talk about our season and what challenged us as we worked our way to the championship, but if I am being honest I kind of want to use this opportunity to talk about something else."

"Like what?"

"I want to talk about my experiences with feeling like I was never good enough in school, on the soccer field or in my life. And I want to share how after my surgery I realized that being enough for society's standards isn't worth my energy anymore. It isn't worth it to loathe the body I am in because it doesn't look like all the models on Instagram or all my favorite characters and actors on TV. It isn't worth it to believe that I am not good enough. We are all good enough just for existing in this world because we have a heart that beats for life and a mind that can do incredible things."

"You know what, I think that is exactly what people need to hear. I am in such awe of you and the growth you have had in just the past week!"

"Thank you, Mom. That means a lot."

"Of course, now you better start writing that speech because the sooner people get to hear what you have to say, the better!"

Five days later, my speech is written, folded up between my hands as I sit next to my mom and dad among the entire student body, waiting to wheel my way up to the stage to share my story. Yes, I said wheel, I have a wheelchair. The crutches were getting really uncomfortable, and if I am being honest, this might be the most comfortable chair I have ever sat in, so I am not complaining.

The principal announces my name and ushers me to the stage, giving me a thumbs up to encourage me to speak my truth. Technically, she doesn't know what truth I am speaking about, but her little sentiment of encouragement was very kind and needed as I look out onto every single student at South Seattle High. Breathing in deeply, I lift my head high and start reading my speech,

"Hi everyone, my name is Hope, for those of you who don't know me. I am a co-captain of the varsity soccer team and I have been asked to talk about our journey to the state championship this year. While I am so proud of my teammates and our hard work that led us there, I want to talk about something else. Something that at first may not sound like it relates to our journeys, but I promise you it relates to mine.

My entire life I have strived to be the best I can be and most of the time to a fault, because I would put immense pressure on myself to succeed and win at everything that I did.

Winning was my measure of success and the definition of my worth. I thought that if I could just get into that honors class or if I could just make it onto varsity then maybe I would feel like I was good enough.

I know that my story may not be exactly like yours, but I know that the desire to feel good enough is shared among all of us. The desire to look like that model on Instagram or be as smart as that one girl in your history class, or be good enough to make that sports team, is something that in one way or another I believe we have all struggled with.

But, I want to talk about the importance of lifting each other up and not giving in to that fear of not measuring up and not being good enough. Because no matter how hard you try you never will be, since the standards of beauty keep changing and the perception of worthiness changes too. So, it is only when you chose yourself over the opinions of others and the voice in your head telling you that you aren't enough, it is only then that you will see you were worthy all along. You were worthy from the day you were born and it's a shame the media doesn't want us to believe that. But I am here to tell you that you are worthy simply because you are alive and breathing. Simply because you got out of bed to live another day even when you had to tell the voice in your head making you think it wasn't worth it, that it was wrong.

I want to share with you that you have the power within you to be who you want to be, without giving in to the idea that you have to change everything about yourself to do so. You don't have to be an all-star player on your soccer team or a straight-A student to be enough, and it took me a long time to believe that. I still have to continue to choose to believe that. But after my injury and after recognizing that it will keep me from playing soccer for a while, and that I won't fit into the typical definition of beauty because of my huge cast and later because of my scar, I realized that the fact that I am breathing and existing in the world makes me good enough. That trendy piece of clothing, that cosmetic surgery, that next big thing the media tells you that you need to be beautiful or worthy is meaningless because I will say it again. You are worthy just as you are. So, I thank you for listening to me and letting me share something that has been on my heart lately. I hope that it inspired you to believe in your incredible uniqueness just a little bit more. Thank you."

The crowd erupts into applause and my hands touch my face in awe of the tremendous response. I smile so wide my cheeks start to hurt, but it doesn't even matter because the fact that I just got up in front of my entire school and shared about my life in its most vulnerable state is everything and more.

The fact that I get to live a life now where I can choose to believe in myself and the truth that I am enough simply because I am, softens any and all pain I endure. I know that choosing myself over the voice in my head and the expectations of who I should be that are ingrained in my being will be difficult. But I am willing to trust that choosing myself over and over again will be the most fulfilling thing I ever do.

Your Journey Forward

Your journey toward awakening to the reality that you are good enough simply because you are begins with your thinking. Changing your thinking about yourself after leading a life where you constantly told yourself or were told that you weren't good enough can be really difficult. Implementing positive affirmations into your life can help ease that difficulty and kickstart your journey toward self-acceptance.

Here are a few suggestions for affirmations that will help lead you on your path to meeting your highest self. And remember, not every day will be the same. Sometimes you may feel like these affirmations aren't helping and you may be tempted to think that there is something wrong with you, but I promise there is absolutely nothing wrong with you. There never was and never will be! Some days you will have to work hard to believe that you are making progress, that you are aligning with your truest self, and most importantly, that you are good enough simply because you are. You've got this and if you don't believe that, just know that I believe in you and know that you are destined for greatness simply because of the extraordinary person you already are.

You can implement these affirmations into your daily morning or night routine, you can repeat them out loud to yourself when you are feeling depressed or anxious, truly anytime you feel called to give your mind and body a little extra love you can turn to these affirmations. I hope they provide you with a basis for the beginning of your self-acceptance journey, but also know that if they aren't your jam that's okay too! Everyone's experience with mental health and working towards accepting themselves is different and I want to stress that that is totally okay. Never feel pressured to do something that doesn't serve you. Your journey is uniquely yours.

Affirmations for Strength

"I am enough simply because I am, no questions asked."

"My worth is not defined by the accolades I acquire, the number of friends I have, or my thoughts on my worst days."

"I believe in myself and my abilities."

"I am stronger than I think I am."

"I have the power to shine my radiant light on the world."

"I am infinitely powerful."

"I am resilient."

"I am free to choose my own reality."

Affirmations for Confidence

"I am enough simply because I am, no questions asked."

"Others opinions of me have no bearing on what I think about myself."

"I accept and love myself unconditionally."

"I have value and I recognize that now."

"I am talented and intelligent in ways unique to me."

"I am worthy of living a life of confidence."

"I am fiercely capable."

"Everything I need is already inside me."

"I trust my intuition."

"I have the ability to believe in my dreams."

"I deserve to be confident in myself because I am incredible."

Affirmations for Anxiety

"I am enough simply because I am, no questions asked."

"My direction is more important than my speed."

"Not everything I think about myself is true, and I recognize that I have the power to change my thinking."

"The universe has my back and everything is working out just as it should be."

"Hope is my guiding light and I trust that I am on the right path."

"I am not my anxious thoughts."

"I trust that this anxiety will pass, and I am not alone in feeling this way."

"I can take things one step at a time."

"I've made it through this feeling before, and I will make it through again."

Affirmations for Body Acceptance

"I am enough simply because I am, no questions asked."

"My body is uniquely mine and that is a pretty special thing."

"My body is supposed to shift, change, and grow with me."

"I accept my body as it is today."

"My worth is not defined by what my body looks like, I define my worth and I am worthy."

"Love fills and touches every inch of my body and I feel that love now."

"I deserve to feel confident and comfortable in my body."

"My body is the vessel that carries my soul through this life, and for that I am grateful."

Communication Is Key

Now that you have had the opportunity to read this book and connect with Hope's journey, taking the time to process what you have read and what you connected with the most is important to jumpstarting your own journey to believing you are enough simply because you are.

Here are a list of questions that will help you better connect with yourself, and to Hope and her story. Ponder these questions and write your response in the spaces provided, and if you are totally in the flow and need more room to write you can always continue your thoughts in a journal. It may also be helpful to talk these questions out in conversation with others who have also interacted with Hope's story.

Communication has the power to show you that you are absolutely not alone in any of your struggles, and it helps you connect with others over a common issue, topic, or idea which is really a powerful thing.

So, refer to these questions to connect with yourself, with Hope, and with others who have read her story, and watch as your understanding of yourself, Hope, and others grows.

Discussion Questions

Do you feel or have you ever felt that you weren't good enough?

_____

_____

_____

_____

_____

_____

What was your biggest takeaway from Hope's story?

_____

_____

_____

_____

_____

_____

What part of Hope's story do you relate to the most? Why? How did it make you feel?

_____

_____

_____

_____

_____

_____

Where do you see yourself in Hope?

_____

_____

_____

_____

_____

Discussion Questions

Addie and Ethan serve as Hope's confidence boosters, who is someone in your life that serves as your confidence booster?

_____

_____

_____

_____

_____

_____

What was your favorite quote from this story? Why did this quote stand out?

_____

_____

_____

_____

_____

_____

What feelings did this book evoke for you?

_____

_____

_____

_____

_____

_____

Would you read another book by this author? Why or why not?

_____

_____

_____

_____

_____

Discussion Questions

If you could ask Hope one question what would it be?

_____

_____

_____

_____

_____

_____

Hope's relationship with her mom is strong and full of love, do you have a relationship in your life resemblant to this bond? If not, that is okay, meaningful relationships take time to develop, just know that you deserve to build a relationship with someone who loves you unconditionally and is willing to lift you up when you are feeling down.

_____

_____

_____

_____

_____

_____

What is the significance of the title? Did you find it meaningful?

_____

_____

_____

_____

_____

_____

_____

_____

_____

Discussion Questions

Did Hope's story change the way you think about yourself or the people around you? How?

_____

_____

_____

_____

_____

_____

What was your favorite chapter and why?

_____

_____

_____

_____

_____

_____

_____

_____

_____

_____

_____

If you could describe Hope's journey in one word, what would it be, and why?

_____

_____

_____

_____

_____

Discussion Questions

How did the setting of this story impact Hope's journey? Do you think her journey would have played out differently in another setting?

_____

_____

_____

_____

_____

_____

What was your initial reaction to the book? Did it take you some time to get into or did it hook you immediately?

_____

_____

_____

_____

_____

_____

What is the main theme you took away from this book?

_____

_____

_____

_____

_____

_____

_____

_____

_____

Journaling Prompts

Journaling is like medicine for the mind. It allows you to see your thoughts on paper and it gives you the opportunity to see which thoughts may be irrational or aren't serving you. Journaling is a wonderful tool that you can use to start to change your thinking patterns, break free from your limiting beliefs, and step into who you want to be.

Here are a few journaling prompts to help aid your journey to self-acceptance and self-love. Use them as you need and allow yourself to fully surrender to the process of expressing your feelings to yourself on paper. It can be hard to see all of the stuff going on in your head, especially if your thoughts are negative and self-deprecating. But, it is important that you know that that is totally okay and totally normal. Growth is not supposed to be easy, you are supposed to come up against hard emotions, but you must allow yourself to feel them so you can move through them and move forward.

When you resist the process of growth, that is where suffering occurs. So, allow yourself to discover the wonder of expressing your feelings on paper, and remember that your journal will never judge you for what you write in it. You are allowed to write about everything and anything that is troubling you because all of your feelings are valid and deserve to be felt.

Start your journey of journaling with the prompts below and observe the powerful shift that occurs in your thinking. You've totally got this!

What are some of your limiting beliefs that might be holding you back?

Write down the type of person you wish to be. Create an avatar, what is their personality? How do they react to difficult situations? How do they live their lives? Think about ways you can bridge the gap between who you are now and the avatar you have created.

_____

_____

_____

_____

_____

_____

_____

_____

_____

_____

_____

_____

_____

_____

_____

_____

_____

_____

_____

_____

_____

_____

_____

_____

_____

_____

Write a love letter to your body thanking it for carrying you and keeping you alive. How does it feel to appreciate your body for what it does for you?

_____

_____

_____

_____

_____

_____

_____

_____

_____

_____

_____

_____

_____

_____

_____

_____

_____

_____

_____

_____

_____

_____

_____

_____

_____

_____

_____

What are you willing to let go of so you can live your fullest life?

What sets your soul on fire, and why do you love yourself for that?

_____

_____

_____

_____

_____

_____

_____

_____

_____

_____

_____

_____

_____

_____

_____

_____

_____

_____

_____

_____

_____

_____

_____

_____

_____

_____

_____

_____

_____

_____

Write a letter to your future self and tell yourself how proud you are for choosing to believe in yourself even when it felt impossible. How does it feel to appreciate your future self in this way?

_____

_____

_____

_____

_____

_____

_____

_____

_____

_____

_____

_____

_____

_____

_____

_____

_____

_____

_____

_____

_____

_____

_____

_____

_____

Do you believe that you are good enough simply because you are? If not, what can you accept about yourself today so that you can start believing that you are good enough, simply because you are?

_____

_____

_____

_____

_____

_____

_____

_____

_____

_____

_____

_____

_____

_____

_____

_____

_____

_____

_____

_____

_____

_____

_____

_____

_____

_____

_____

CPSIA information can be obtained
at www.ICGtesting.com
Printed in the USA
BVHW041033100721
611579BV00016B/1092

9 781087 874425